Erin

For Mom: who raised me to be relentlessly curious
and to crave my artistic dreams.

EM

For Dad: who taught me to be brave.

Library of Congress Cataloging-in-Publication Data available.

ISBN: 978-1-7343928-0-7

www.thecultivatedgroup.co

Esmè
the Curious Cat.

Written By: EM Valentine
Illustrated By: Erin Spencer

You see Esmè, she is a curious cat,
with global adventures that are fueled by just that.

By her instincts she's led as she wanders and plays,
approaching the world with a wide-open gaze.
She defines the adventure and creates her own luck,
knowing deeply to no one else she can pass the buck.

She doesn't eat cheese
and she doesn't like milk.
This peculiar, cute cat
really likes to wear silk.

She isn't quite black
and she isn't quite white,

Esmè walks on two legs
with imperfect eye-sight.

She traipses the world with one rule in mind,
the single most important thing is to be kind.
Be kind to your playmates and be kind to your friends,
even when disappointed only love and light she sends.

She belongs nowhere and everywhere, they're one in the same,
with the deep understanding that life can be a playful game.

She skips and she hops,
all the way up mountain-tops!

She swings and she slides,
through her playground she glides.

And the more she sees,
the more she knows,
the more she learns,
the more she grows.

The more she adventures and the more that she sees,
the more Esmè learns the world needs bigger dreams!
Her imagination simply can't help but take flight,
she just can't believe the possibilities in sight!

Fiercely independent yet never alone,
embraced by warm welcome
wherever she calls home.

From sunrises top-mountain
to saving turtles at the beach,
she'll share lessons learned
to further her life's reach.

See, this great, great big world
isn't that big at all.
Once you see what she's seen,
you'll realize it's really quite small.

You see, life's an adventure if you choose to engage,
the rest still unwritten — including the next page.

And the thing is we're all connected,
if not simply by heart,

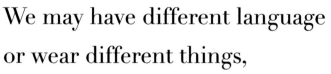

by this one great big world
of which we all are a part.

We may have different language
or wear different things,

But all know the love, joy,
and light kindness brings.

In a world full of darkness
we must not lose sight.

There is so much good
and that good shines SO bright!

On her journeys she'll take you through the rain and the snow,
but in your life only YOU will choose the direction you'll go.
The world is her playground and it's your playground too,
the only one writing your story will be you.

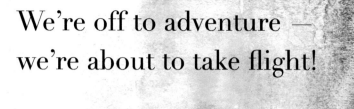

We're off to adventure —
we're about to take flight!

Quick, quick, quick —

come along with us.

choose your joy — spread your light!